Uncle Rocky
Fireman

BOOK #1

"FIRE!"

James Burd Brewster

As told to Ben and Luke by their father, James Burd Brewster

Written by James Burd Brewster

Illustrated by Dayna Barley-Cohrs

J2B Publishing LLC, Pomfret, MD

Written By - James Burd Brewster

Illustrations By - Dayna Barley-Cohrs

Design / Layout By - James Burd Brewster and Dayna Barley-Cohrs

Published By - J2B Publishing LLC

Copyright 2013 by James Burd Brewster (text)
www.GladToDoIt.net

Copyright 2013 Dayna Barley-Cohrs (art)
www.daynabarleycohrs.ca

ISBN: 978-0-9911994-1-9

What people are saying about Uncle Rocky, Fireman:

"I love your books. Ben usually has a very whining attitude when I ask him to do something. Not lately. Well, not since we bought your books. Now, when I ask him to do something he pauses and says "Glad to do it". I love it. It's such a joy to hear. Thank you."

- - Kristen Tidwell

"We have read through your lovely book several times now. It's a very sweet story, yet with lots of great mechanical details that are sweet sounds to curious little boys. The part about the baby being in potential danger always tugs at a parent's emotions ..... When I asked Win (5 yr old son) what he liked best about the story it was 'when he saved the baby.' Mine too :)"

- - Katherine Shepler

Author's Note:

I hope you enjoy reading Uncle Rocky, Fireman Book #1 - Fire! with your children as much as I enjoyed telling it to my boys.

Uncle Rocky, Fireman is a series of stories I told to my two oldest sons in 1989 and 1990 when they were 4.5 and 6. My boys quickly memorized the sequence of events initiated by the alarm bell and developed hand and body motions that pantomimed getting dressed for the fire. They enjoyed making the sounds of starting the truck and testing the horn. They looked like traffic cops when they held up their hands to stop traffic so the fire truck could race to the fire. The best part was the ending when they mimicked Uncle Rocky as he said, "Glad to do it!"

Author's Acknowledgements:

This book would not be possible without:

- Ben and Luke, my eager boys, who made telling these stories so much fun.
- Katie, my loving wife, who created the environment where I could tell these stories and who tells me each Uncle Rocky rough draft is "Great" even though we know better.
- Dayna, whose illustrations have brought Uncle Rocky to life exactly as Luke had always imagined.

Rocky Hill's third week of duty as a fireman began early on Monday. His training and practice were over. He really was a fireman. At the station, he checked in at the radio desk, and walked by the chief's office.

"Morning, Chief," he said.

"Good to see you Rocky," answered the chief in a voice made harsh by smoke inhalation.

Uncle Rocky went to his bunk and put his bag under the bed. Then he made sure his helmet, boots, turnout coat, and pants were ready on the equipment rack.

He joined up with Big Joe, the driver, and Bob, the Captain, of the hook-and-ladder truck. Uncle Rocky was the tillerman, the driver at the rear of the truck.

The three had just debriefed the fire crew that was going off-duty and were having coffee in the kitchen upstairs when...

The alarm bell rang!

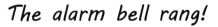

CLANG CLANG!!
CLANG CLANG CLANG!!

Uncle Rocky, Bob, and Big Joe ran to the pole and slid down through the floor to the dressing racks waiting there.

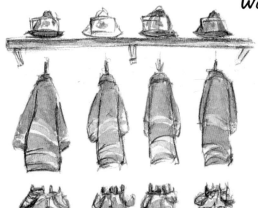

Rocky put his feet through his turnout pants and into his boots, pulling them on one at a time,

first the right boot,

then the left.

He pulled up his turnout pants and put the suspenders over his shoulders, first the right strap, then the left.

His turnout coat came next.

Uncle Rocky put his arms into the sleeves, first the right arm, then the left.

He fastened the snaps up the front:

snap, snap...

snap,

snap,

snap.

He grabbed his helmet, put it on his head, and pulled down the face shield.

Fully clothed and ready for any fire, Uncle Rocky scrambled to his position at the rear steering wheel.

Big Joe started the truck.

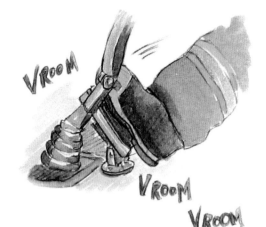

VROOM

VROOM VROOM

Voo Voo Voo

Bob flipped on the lights,

He flicked on the siren.

WHIRR WHIRR WHIRR

Big Joe tested the air horn.

ENNNT ENNNT

The chief told Big Joe the alarm came in from Ingleside road. The traffic light outside the station turned red, traffic stopped, and the big doors swung open.

The hook-and-ladder truck pulled out of the station and raced to the fire.

They roared up Belair road, across Northern Parkway,
up Harford road, and made a left onto Ingleside.
Rocky steered perfectly.

Before they had even arrived, Uncle Rocky could smell the smoke and knew they would soon be facing a serious fire. People needed his help and he was ready!

Bob pulled the truck to a stop in front of a two-story house. Smoke and flames were pouring out of the second story windows. A young lady rushed up to them, crying:

"My baby! My baby! She's still inside. Please save my baby!"

Uncle Rocky, Bob, and Big Joe sprang into action.

"No ladder," shouted Bob. "We'll fight this inside. Big Joe, take a hose through the front door. Rocky, you go for the baby."

Big Joe put on his oxygen tank, grabbed a hose, and ran toward the house. Bob hooked up the main hose to the fire hydrant and Uncle Rocky started the pumps.

Big Joe went in the front door and bounded up the stairs. At the top, he saw the smoke and felt the flames. He braced himself to fight the fire.

He pulled the lever on the fire hose nozzle and water streamed out: *foossch!*

He pointed the water stream at the ceiling first. The water doused the flames and fell to the floor like a shower, putting out more flames on the way down. Big Joe swept the water along the walls from the ceiling to the floor. The hallway fire was soon under control.

Uncle Rocky put on his oxygen tank and faced the frantic young woman. Uncle Rocky's heart began to pound with the urgency of the situation.

"I'll get your baby, Ma'am. Where is she?"

"On the second floor, in the back bedroom. She was taking a nap in her crib. Please save her," she pleaded.

Uncle Rocky patted her arm and sprinted for the door of the house. He took the steps two at a time. Upstairs the smoke was still very thick. He brushed past Big Joe who was going into the front bedroom.

Uncle Rocky dropped to the floor where the smoke was thinner and looked for the back bedroom. With relief, he noticed the flames had stayed in the front of the house, so the baby was not in danger from the flames. But in this smoke, the baby could die from the lack of oxygen.

"Got to get to her quickly," he thought.

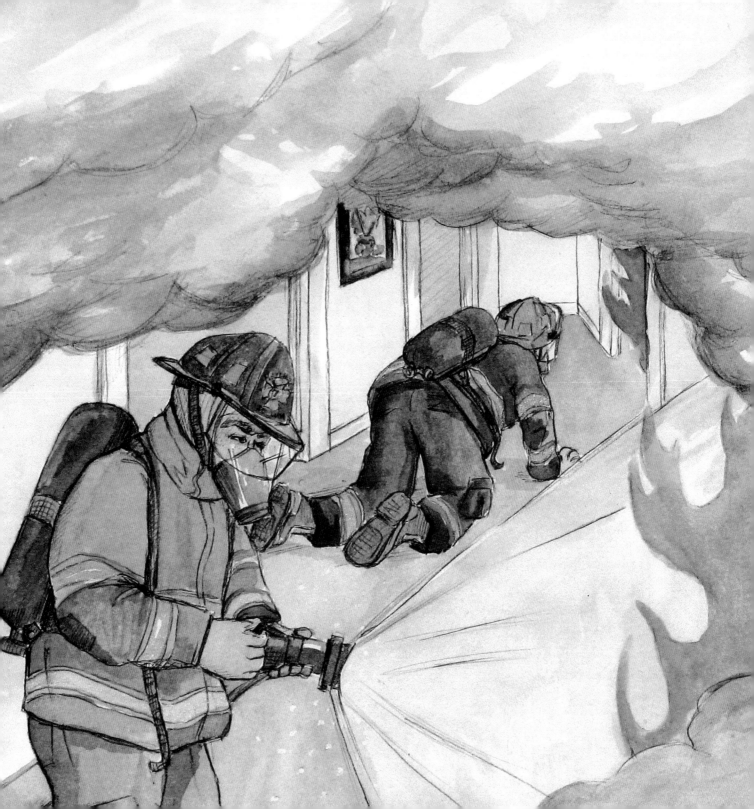

Big Joe put the nozzle on 'spray,' moved to the bedroom door, and stuck the nozzle through the doorway. The wide spray instantly reduced the intensity of the fire in the room.

Big Joe advanced inside and repeated the same method he used in the hallway. He attacked the fire on the ceiling first and let the falling shower of water and debris help fight the rest of the fire.

Uncle Rocky crawled into the first bedroom on his left and noticed a twin bed.

Wrong room!

Quickly, he backed out and crawled to the next room. He noticed baby toys on the floor.

This must be it!

Crawling through the room, he felt the legs of a crib, reached into it, and touched a baby. The baby did not move.

"Uncle Rocky picked up the baby, covered her with his arms, and held her close to his chest and turnout coat.

He raced through the hallway and down the stairs to fresh air. Uncle Rocky was worried. The baby still had not moved.

Outside, the young lady tried to run up to Uncle Rocky, but Bob kept her back until Uncle Rocky could examine the baby.

Uncle Rocky opened his arms. He looked at the baby and gave a big sigh of relief.

He smiled, walked over to the mother, and gently placed the baby in her arms. She smiled and started to cry. Her daughter was sound asleep.

The mother looked up at Uncle Rocky with tears in her eyes and said, "Thank you. Thank you for saving my baby. Thank God you came in time."

Uncle Rocky felt good. He also thanked God. This is why he had become a firefighter.

He looked into the mother's eyes and said,

"Glad to do it!"

Tomorrow night: Rocky Hill, Fireman "Something's Missing"

James Burd Brewster was raised in Albany, NY, learned to sail on Lake Champlain, navigated a Polar Icebreaker in the US Coast Guard, and married Katie Spivey from Wilmington, NC. They lived in Baltimore, MD when Ben and Luke heard the Rocky Hill, Fireman stories. The family grew to five (Ben, Luke, Rachel, Andrew, Sam) and settled in Pomfret, MD outside of Washington, DC. Ben and Luke are no longer 6 and 4. Ben is a Marine, married, and father of four. Luke is an Apple employee in Chicago, IL. Ben now tells Uncle Rocky stories to his sons, Levi, Micah, and Judah.

Children can contact Uncle Rocky and James Burd Brewster through www.gladtodoit.net

Dayna Barley-Cohrs lives in a secluded straw bale home in the small village of Vankoughnet, Ontario, Canada. Trained at the Ontario College of Art and Design in Fine Arts, with a focus on figurative and portrait work, she works as a freelance illustrator and fine artist. She is the mother of two young children, whom she loves to draw pictures for and finds useful as art critics. Dayna and her artist husband also homestead as much as they can, when not working in the studio she can be found growing food, raising chickens and bees, and canning the harvest. In her spare time, she sleeps. Dayna was found and commissioned for these illustrations through Elance.com.

Made in the USA
Charleston, SC
14 January 2014